Edited by Deborah Campbell-Todd
Designed by Oxprint Ltd

ISBN 0 86112 748 X
Published by Brimax Books Ltd, Newmarket, England 1991.
Second printing 1991.
Printed in Hong Kong.

ROONEY
to the Rescue

by Lucy Kincaid
Illustrated by Eric Kincaid

Brimax Books · Newmarket · England

A Find

Will had taken his tool bag to a house in the village. A handle had come off a cupboard door and it was also loose on its hinges. Tiny Miss Smith wanted it fixed.

Rooney went along with Will to keep him company and to run errands, for Will that is, not Miss Smith.

Miss Smith had taken everything out of the cupboard to make it easier to do the job.

"This should only take a few minutes," said Will. "All it needs is a couple of new screws."

Rooney was standing inside the cupboard, holding a hinge while Will screwed it, when Miss Smith opened a downstairs window. A strong draught blew up the stairs and caught the door. It blew it shut with a bang, with Rooney on the inside, Will on the outside, and no handle on the door in between to open it.

"Let me out!" shouted Rooney banging on the door. "It's dark in here, I don't like it."

"Don't worry, have you out in a jiffy," said Will.

All he had to do was undo a few screws.

That was easier said than done with Miss Smith twittering about under his elbow and getting in the way, and with Rooney shouting and banging from inside the cupboard. He found it hard to concentrate on what he was doing. It took him rather longer than a jiffy to get the screws out.

Miss Smith was making so much noise outside the cupboard that Will failed to notice that the noise coming from inside the cupboard had stopped.

"Out you come," he said, when the door was open.

"Where's he gone?" twittered Miss Smith poking her head into the cupboard. "I didn't see him come out."

"That's because he hasn't come out," said Will.

"Then where is he?" twittered Miss Smith.

"Stop playing jokes, Rooney," said Will, looking into the cupboard himself, quite expecting to see Rooney's eyes peeping through his tail from one of the dark corners.

But he wasn't there. The cupboard was empty.

"Hallo," called a faint voice from far, far away.

"Rooney! Is that you?" called Will. But Rooney, if it was Rooney, didn't answer.

"I'd better get Pa," said Will, looking worried.

"No, no, you stay and find Rooney, I'll go for Pa," said Miss Smith and went quickly down the stairs.

While she was gone Will got the light out of the tool bag and shone it into every dark corner. He tapped round all the walls to see whether there was a secret panel that Rooney might have disappeared through. If there was one, he couldn't find it.

9

Presently Pa came leaping up the stairs two at a time.

"Have you found him?" he gasped.

"No," said Will. "I'm worried."

It was Pa who found the gap between the floorboards. He accidentally put his foot in it.

"That's big enough for Rooney to fall through," he said.

He got onto his knees and called through the gap.

"Rooney! Are you there? Answer me!"

"Hallo!" called Rooney's voice from far, far away.

"Help! Help!" Suddenly there was a scream and a shattering crash from somewhere downstairs.

Pa and Will found Miss Smith standing in the pantry with smashed plates and basins, and rice pudding, and boiled potatoes, and squashed tomatoes round her feet.

She was very pale. Her eyes were big and round. She was pointing to the wall in front of her. She tried to say something but she couldn't.

Will went just as pale as

Miss Smith when he saw what she was pointing out. His eyes went big and round, too.

There was a little grill set into the pantry wall. It was put there to let the air in and keep the pantry fresh. Looking through it were two shining eyes.

"There was no need to scream," said a plaintive voice. "It's only me."

It was Rooney.

"How did you get in there?" asked Will, putting his face so close to the grill the end of his nose poked through it.

Rooney started to explain, but Pa said, "Questions and answers later, let's get him out first."

"That is a very good idea," said Rooney.

Pa cleared everything off the pantry shelf that hadn't been knocked off by Miss Smith, then unscrewed the grill.

Seconds later a dusty, cobwebby, and excited Rooney stepped out onto the shelf.

"I think you'd better explain yourself," said Pa.

"I've had an adventure. I've found a secret staircase!" said Rooney.

"Secret staircase!" That news brought Miss Smith out of her trance. "Secret staircase? In my house? Where?"

"Behind there," said Rooney, pointing to the wall behind him.

"Knock it down . . . knock it down . . . NOW . . ." Miss Smith was VERY excited and VERY eager.

Pa and Will were just as keen to see it as she was so they set to work there and then. Soon the pantry, and everything and everyone in it, was covered with dust, and there was a hole in the wall big enough for them all to get through.

They could see a narrow, winding staircase, going upwards.

"I know the way, I'll go first," said Rooney before anyone else had a chance to get in front of him.

At the top their way was barred by wooden boards. Rooney squeezed his way through a gap between them and disappeared.

"We'll never get through there," said Will, looking over Pa's shoulder."

"We won't have to," said Pa. "It's a trapdoor."

Pa pushed with his shoulders and moved the trapdoor to one side. They went up the last few steps and found themselves standing, like sardines in a can, inside the cupboard Will had been mending earlier and from which Rooney had so mysteriously disappeared.

Miss Smith showed all her visitors the secret staircase. They were always very surprised when they went into the cupboard at the top of the stairs and came out into the pantry downstairs. It soon became the secret staircase that EVERYONE knew about.

The Glue Brush

"Oh bother," said Aunt Tilda crossly.

She had dropped her sewing box and everything had fallen out. Cotton reels had rolled across the floor. Pins had stuck into the carpet like a broken down fence. Buttons had spilled in a cascade. Aunt Tilda got to her knees and started to pick things up. She didn't like muddles of any sort. This kind of muddle she liked even less, it made her cross.

She began to fix the compartments back into her sewing box and discovered that it had broken in the fall.

14

"Oh no!" she cried in dismay. Her sewing box was very old. It had belonged to her grandmother. It was very important to her. She forgot all about the muddle on the floor. She gathered the pieces of her box together and without bothering to put on her coat or her hat, or even to change into her outdoor shoes, she hurried to the workshop.

"Whatever is wrong?" asked Pa. He wasn't used to seeing Aunt Tilda so close to tears.

"It's my box," she said. "It's broken . . . please . . . can you mend it for me?"

"Give it here," said Pa. "Let me look." He laid the pieces on the bench and moved them around while Aunt Tilda looked on anxiously.

"Nothing here that a bit of glue won't fix," said Pa. "Glue pot please, Rooney."

Rooney brought the glue pot and Pa put it to warm on the little stove that he kept at the back of the bench. The glue had to be melted before it would stick The way to do that was to make it warm. Pa always did that himself. He wouldn't let anyone else touch the glue pot when it was hot.

"Glue brush, please Rooney," said Pa when the glue was neither too hot, nor too cold, but just right.

Rooney fetched it from its place on the brush rack. Pa dipped it in the glue and then while Will held two of the broken pieces for him, he carefully painted the edges with the glue. When he had finished he gave Rooney the brush to hold, took the two pieces from Will and pressed them together. It had to be done carefully and it took time.

Rooney was so intent on getting his nose under Aunt Tilda's nose so that he could see what Pa and Will were doing, he didn't watch what HE was doing with the brush. Somehow it got too close to Aunt Tilda's skirt. Will saw what had happened and secretly came to the rescue.

The glue was sticky and stretchy like treacle and pulled pieces of fluff from Aunt Tilda's skirt.

Meanwhile Pa had sorted out two more pieces of the box and was ready for the glue brush again.

"Brush," he said, talking to Rooney, but looking at what he was doing.

Rooney was worried about the sticky patch on

Aunt Tilda's skirt. He still wasn't looking at what he
was doing himself.

"Ugh!" said Pa as he found himself holding
a handful of sticky bristles.

"Oh . . . er sorry," said Rooney. He and Pa had
a tug of war with the brush.

"Behave yourselves!" tutted Aunt Tilda. "This is
no time to play games."

"I'm not playing games," said Pa.

"Neither am I," said Rooney.

Pa did the next bit of the glueing.

He hesitated before giving the brush back to
Rooney.

"Be careful with it this time," he said sternly.

Aunt Tilda glared at Rooney. Rooney couldn't
help seeing the sticky patch on her skirt no matter how

17

hard he tried not to. He decided it might be safer to put the brush down before he did something else silly with it. There was still some glue in the bristles so he couldn't lay it down on top of anything. Then he had an idea. He wedged the handle of the brush between two planks of wood. It stood up like a stubby, sticky tree.

"It can't stick to anyone there," thought Rooney with relief.

"Brush," said Pa presently. "Brush please," said Pa again.

Rooney had heard him the first time and was looking about him in a panic. "It's gone," he gasped.

"What do you mean? Gone!" said Pa.

"Gone gone," said Rooney. "It's vanished!"

Will took a quick look at the back of Aunt Tilda's skirt and breathed a sigh of relief. At least it wasn't stuck there.

"It's not gone anywhere," said Aunt Tilda. "It's right behind you."

"Where?" said Rooney, twirling like a spinning top.

"Ouch!" said Aunt Tilda as something hard hit her sharply on the shins.

"Ouch!" said Will, as something equally hard hit him just as sharply on his shins.

"Stand still!" ordered Pa sternly.

As Rooney stopped twirling something hard hit
him from behind. Without him noticing, his tail had
touched the sticky end of the brush and now the brush
was dangling from the end of his tail like a wooden
leg.

"Get it off!" he shouted. "Ouch!" he shouted as Pa
pulled.

His tail and the brush had been touching longer
than anyone realized. The glue on the brush had had
time to harden. Tail and brush were well and truly
stuck together.

"Soften the glue with water," said Aunt Tilda.

Rooney sat with his tail in a bucket of water for

ages. All that happened was his tail got wet and he got stiff with sitting still for so long. The brush and his tail would not part company.

Rooney began to think of all the things he couldn't do with a brush sticking to the end of his tail.

"It will have to be cut off," said Aunt Tilda, and she reached for the scissors.

"Don't let her do it," pleaded Rooney. "Please don't let her cut my tail off."

"Silly raccoon!" said Aunt Tilda. "Catch him!" she ordered Pa as Rooney tried to run away. "Hold him still!"

Snip! Snip! went the scissors. To Rooney's surprise he felt no pain. He had been sure it would hurt when his tail was cut off, but of course his tail WASN'T cut off.

Aunt Tilda had just cut away the brush. Some of the long hairs from the end of his tail were still sticking to the brush and some of the hairs on his tail were very much shorter than they had been, but that was all. What a relief it was.

Aunt Tilda took charge of the glue brush herself after that and then there was no more trouble with it.

"Thank you," said Aunt Tilda when the box was finally mended.

"It took longer than I expected," . . . everyone looked at Rooney and he looked at his toes . . . "but thank you just the same."

As for Rooney. He vowed that the next time Pa called for the glue brush he would find something to keep him busy at the other end of the woodshed.

To the Rescue

"Help! Help!" Rooney came running into the woodshed, whiskers trembling and tail streaming.

Will looked up from his saw. Pa looked up from his chisel.

"What is it?" they asked.

Rooney's words came tumbling out of his mouth in a jumble.

"Rab . . . tre . . . cli . . . fall . . . riv . . . hur . . . qui . . ."

They couldn't understand a word he was saying and he didn't have time to say it all over again.

"Come with me . . . ," he said instead, and disappeared through the door in a cloud of dust.

"I think we'd better," said Pa putting down his chisel.

"I think you could be right," said Will putting down his saw.

Even with their long legs it took them a while to catch up with Rooney. His little legs were moving very fast.

"Hurry . . . do hurry . . . ," he kept saying. "Hurry . . . before something dreadful happens."

Rooney led them to the river bank. Clinging for dear life to a high branch overhanging the water was a rabbit.

Will rubbed his eyes and looked again.

"What is a rabbit doing up there?" asked Pa in astonishment.

"Someone dared him," said Rooney. "Someone said rabbits couldn't climb and he said he'd show them, and he did, but now he's stuck. You've got to get him down before he falls into the river. He can't swim. If he falls into the river he will drown."

Will didn't really see why. If he was clever enough to climb he was probably clever enough to swim. But the rabbit was tired of being clever. He just wanted to be rescued.

Will climbed up the tree. The branches were a bit thin. They had a nasty way of bouncing as he edged further along them.

"You're too heavy!" shouted Pa. "Come back before you break the branch and you both fall into the river."

Will was glad to have his feet back on firm ground. But that didn't get the rabbit out of the tree.

"Come and get me . . . ," pleaded the rabbit.

"Can't you climb back on your own?" asked Will.

"I'm frightened," said the rabbit. "I'm used to being on the ground. I don't know what to do."

"We'll have to think of something," said Pa.

Pa had an idea. He stepped down from the bank into the rushing river water. He waded across the stony bottom until he was standing directly beneath the rabbit.

He held up his arms.

"Let go . . . ," he said. "I'll catch you . . ."

"I can't!" squealed the rabbit. "I'm afraid."

"You've got too!" shouted Rooney . . . "Or you'll never get down."

But the rabbit wouldn't move.

"This is ridiculous," said Will as Pa waded back to the bank. "A rabbit shouldn't be in a tree anyway."

"Whether he should, or whether he shouldn't, he is," said Pa.

"And we've got to do something about it."

"Stand on my shoulders and we'll try to lift him down," said Pa. It sounded simple enough. Pa crouched down so that Will could step straight from the bank to his shoulders.

Carefully, oh so carefully, Pa stretched up and began to walk back into the river.

The trouble was, Pa was walking over stones that hurt his feet and made him wobble.

The trouble was, Will had nothing at all to hold onto. After one last frantic wobble when he tried to catch hold of the sky he overbalanced. Pa overbalanced with him.

SPLASH!!! Water shot into the air like a fountain. It soaked the rabbit high in the tree. It fell back onto the heads of Pa and Will as they found themselves sitting in water that came up to their chins.

They were too busy spluttering to notice what happened next. If they had they would have seen Rooney race up into the tree and along the thin bouncy branch.

Rooney had been thinking. He knew what to do now.

"Now listen to me and do exactly as I say," he said to the rabbit. "I will tell you where to put your feet, and what to hold onto."

"But I will fall," sobbed the rabbit.

"Not if I'm holding you," said Rooney. He was edging backwards, and getting closer and closer to the rabbit.

"Don't come any closer . . . you'll tickle my nose . . . you'll make me sneeze . . . and then I'll go

27

crashing to the ground," squealed the rabbit.

"Don't be silly," said Rooney. "I'm going to wrap my tail round you and hold you."

And if Pa and Will had been looking they would have seen the rabbit, wearing Rooney's tail round his middle like a ruff, edge slowly inch by inch along that dangerous, springy, bouncy, branch.

Twice the rabbit put his foot in the wrong place and began to slip. Each time Rooney tightened his tail round the rabbit. Each time he held on tightly himself. And each time the danger passed. At last they were both safely on the ground.

What Pa and Will did see when they had stopped spluttering was Rooney and the rabbit standing side by side on the bank laughing at them.

28

Pa looked first at the rabbit, then at the empty branch above his head and then back at the rabbit.

"How did you get there?" he asked.

"He probably flew," said Will. "I wouldn't put anything past that rabbit. He's probably an elephant in disguise."

The rabbit told them how Rooney had come to his rescue.

"Why didn't you do that in the first place?" asked Will.

"I didn't think of it," said Rooney, "or I would have."

"Next time there's an emergency, think before you get excited," said Pa, wiping drips of river water from his eyebrows. "Then you might save us all a lot of trouble."